# Chapter One

On the last day of the holiday, Claire woke early. In the soft bed beside her, Anthony snored quietly. He was a big man and took up most of the bed. One long leg and an arm were totally on Claire's side, but she didn't mind. She watched him for a moment, smiling at the way his dark hair was messily tangled in sleep. His skin was smooth and brown against the cool white of the sheets. Unlike hers, she thought.

Claire was as pale as a milk bottle, no matter how much Greek sun she got. During their two weeks on the beautiful island of Corfu, she'd slowly moved from sunscreen Factor 25 down to Factor 8. She'd sunbathed for four hours one day, nearly falling asleep on the beach as the sea lapped gently against the shore. It had made no difference, except that her freckles had sort of joined up. With his dark brown eyes and rich tan, Anthony could have been a local.

She slipped out from under the sheets, moving quietly so as not to wake her sleeping husband. At home, she never woke until her alarm clock blasted morning radio into her ears. Here in

Greece, she woke at six most days. It was the light. On Corfu, the sun was magical. It beamed into the small blue and white hotel bedroom, urging her to wake up and enjoy the day.

In the quiet suburb where she and Anthony lived in Ireland, you could count the days when the sun sneaked in past the heavy brocade curtains and into their bedroom. But here in Greece, sunlight was part of the experience. It made the white walls gleam, made the sea glitter. It made Claire Reynolds feel so very happy.

Still barefoot and in pale blue pyjama shorts and T-shirt, Claire gently opened the pine balcony doors and stepped outside. Hotel Athena was a sprawling, white, two-storey building, a quarter of a mile from the beach. The brochure had said it was a five-minute walk away and for once, the travel brochure hadn't lied.

In fact, the brochure hadn't done Hotel Athena justice:

*Simple Greek hotel noted for its hospitality and quietness, with a beautiful garden behind the hotel where guests can sample traditional Greek cooking.*

This hadn't described the pure kindness of Sarah, the lovely English lady who ran the hotel with her Greek husband, Stavros. When their coach dropped off Claire and Anthony and the other Irish guests, Sarah welcomed them all as if they were beloved relatives she hadn't seen for years. If she felt they were the hugging kind, she hugged them.

Sarah was short and round, with long wavy blonde hair that was going grey. She wore a flowing light cotton dress that seemed to be made up of pink and purple flowers. Her many silver bangles jangled as she walked. Smiling and chattering, she led them into the hotel's cool, flower-scented lobby and made them sit down on blue-striped couches. Stavros, who was tall and dark and smiled a lot, offered trays of freshly squeezed orange juice or the local brandy. He didn't speak, just watched his wife fondly.

When everyone was sitting, Sarah organised the rooms according to what she thought they needed.

'You,' she said, standing back and narrowing her eyes at Claire and Anthony, 'need the honey-moon suite.'

Claire had laughed out loud. 'We're not on honeymoon,' she said truthfully, finding Anthony's hand and squeezing it. She'd have loved a honeymoon suite, but it wouldn't have been right to lie about it. At this point in her life, thirty-three last birthday, Claire liked total honesty.

'Oh, I know you're not just married,' Sarah said, smiling, 'but I have a honeymoon feeling about you two. People in love need the honeymoon suite. You agree, Stavros?'

Stavros nodded and began to look for their suitcases. Before Claire and Anthony knew it, they were being led up a winding wooden staircase to a pretty white and blue room with a jug of pink flowers sitting on the pine dressing table. The big double bed was made up with frilled snowy-white pillows and a duvet that looked as soft as a cloud. There were two blue-striped armchairs like the couches in the lobby, and several watercolour paintings on the wall. The paintings were of pink and purple flowers like the ones on Sarah's dress.

Stavros showed them the little bathroom with its gleaming white tiles.

He didn't have to say 'Do you like it?' because Claire's face told him she liked it. There was no television and no minibar stuffed full of tiny bottles of gin or vodka. Just a small kettle on a tray with tea and coffee things, and a bottle of mineral water. There was also a feeling of utter peace. As if nothing bad could ever happen to anyone in this lovely room. It felt like a sanctuary, which was exactly what Claire and Anthony had come to Greece to find.

'Thank you,' Claire said gratefully. 'It's lovely. Don't you think so, darling?' she asked Anthony.

Anthony, who'd been tense since Stavros had passed him with a tray bearing glasses of brandy earlier, nodded. He sat down on one of the armchairs, stretched out his long legs and breathed deeply, like a man who'd just reached land after being lost in the sea.

'It's lovely,' he said slowly.

His eyes met Claire's. They understood each other perfectly. It would be easier not to feel tempted to drink in this room. Anthony would not have to sit on the balcony and think of the bottles of vodka calling his name from the minibar. Here, there was hope.

In the warm light of their last full day on the island, Claire remembered how happy she'd felt the first day.

Sarah had been right: it was sort of a honeymoon for them. A new start. A life without Anthony drinking.

From the balcony, Claire could see a few people walking on the beach. The man from the little cafe beside the beach was busily washing down his terrace floor. The lady in the souvenir shop next door was setting up her racks outside: lots of colourful buckets and spades for the children, and huge blow-up things for the swimming pools. There were dinosaurs in acid greens, and squashy Barbie-pink armchairs. Claire loved watching the children on the beach. She adored the way the small ones ran giggling into the waves, then rushed out squealing when the water 'got' them.

She'd made friends with another Irish woman on the beach who had two young children. Tricia was a little older than Claire and the two women had bonded as they sat in the sun. Tricia set up camp on the sand every day with a pile of towels, lots of suncream, several base-ball hats and a ready supply of hugs. Claire liked sitting beside her and chatting. The two children rushed up every few minutes looking for plasters or an ice cream.

'Mummy, Fiona says there's a *huge* shark in the sea!' the little one, Millie, would scream.

Millie was five. Behind her, seven-year-old Fiona would grin naughtily.

'Only a small shark, Mum,' she'd say.

'Don't tease her,' Tricia would reply calmly. Millie would get a kiss, another bit of suncream on her neck, and be sent off. Tricia watched them constantly. She had a magazine on her lap, but Claire never saw her read it.

Five minutes later, the two little girls would come back with a supply of shells.

'I want to build a sandcastle,' Fiona would announce. 'Give me my bucket.'

'*Please* may I have my bucket,' Tricia would correct.

Fiona, who was blonde, adorable and knew it, would roll her eyes. '*Please may I have my bucket, Mummy,*' she'd groan.

Tricia's husband, Pat, was like Anthony in that he liked to read in the sun. Between them, they read book after book. They both loved American thrillers and spent ages talking about them. But at lunchtime, Pat liked a beer with his lunch. So Anthony stayed on the beach to read.

'If you get any browner, they won't let you leave the country: they'll think you're Greek,' Pat joked one day, when he'd had a few beers and his pleasant face was tinged with red. 'Are you sure you won't come up and have a bottle of beer with me?'

Claire held her breath.

'Ah no, Pat,' Anthony said, 'beer in the sun doesn't agree with me.'

'You see, Pat, *somebody's* sensible about not drinking too much in the sun,' Tricia said to her husband, patting his beer belly.

Claire breathed again. The moment had passed.

At night, Tricia, Pat and the children ate early. This gave Anthony and Claire the perfect excuse not to go to dinner with them. Without ever speaking about it, Claire knew how hard it would be for her husband to watch Pat drink lots of wine with his meal.

One morning, Pat had a terrible hangover after the night before.

'There's a brass band in my head,' he groaned, sinking on to the sun lounger and shading his eyes from the sun. 'That sun's very bright, isn't it?'

'The sun's normal. You've got a headache because of the five Long Island Iced Tea cocktails you had,' said Tricia crossly. 'I told you not to drink them. You're lucky you're not married to a big idiot,' she added to Claire.

They both looked down to the water where Anthony was playing in the sea with Millie and Fiona. He was pretending to be a shark chasing them out of the shallow waves. Every time he chased them, the two little girls squealed with delight.

He was slim and handsome, with no sign of a beer belly. He'd been going to the gym at home and his stomach was flat and muscled.

In his denim-blue swimming shorts, with his dark hair windswept, he could have stepped out of a film.

Claire felt her heart ache watching him play with the girls. Anthony had never played with children much before. At family gatherings, he hadn't wanted to play with her nieces and nephews. Instead, he'd sat with the men and the drinks, talking and smoking. Now she watched his face alight with happiness as he pretended to be a shark for two small girls.

'I'm very lucky,' she said, and it was the truth.

# Chapter Two

On the last morning of her holiday, Jessica made herself her cup of coffee with the special little filter-coffee containers she'd brought from home. It was strange how something so small could give a person so much pleasure. She usually didn't buy them because they were expensive. No, she corrected herself. It wasn't the expense. She usually didn't buy them because they were a treat.

The grief counsellor, Diana, had said it was important to be honest. Diana was the one who'd pointed out that the reason Jessica didn't do nice things for herself had nothing to do with money. She had enough money to survive. Jack's life insurance meant she'd never go hungry. She didn't buy magazines or perfume, or go for a facial in the beautician's because they were treats. It was as if Jessica wasn't allowed to do anything nice for herself ever again.

Jack was dead and so was all the happiness in Jessica's life.

'You *can* live your life like that,' Diana had

said bluntly during their third session. Blunt speaking seemed to be Diana's speciality. There had been no mention of such bluntness in her advert. The very name 'grief counsellor' had implied a kind person who somehow magically made you feel better. Not someone who forced you to think painful thoughts. 'But there's no *need* to live like that,' Diana said. 'There's no need to keep on punishing yourself because you're alive and Jack's dead. You can have nice meals, buy yourself a magazine every now and then, and enjoy yourself with friends. You're not betraying him. You're simply punishing yourself by not doing those things. You must ask yourself why.'

Jessica was shocked. In the two years since Jack had died a painful death from pancreatic cancer, nobody had spoken to her like that. The death of your beloved husband changed all your relationships. People spoke to you as if *you* were the person who was ill. They spoke in gentle voices and asked if you were *'all right'*. They said things like *'under the circumstances . . .'*

Under the circumstances, it was perfectly normal not to go to parties or weddings. It was normal not to want to get your hair done, normal not to buy new clothes. It was normal to buy the cheapest instant coffee in the super-market because it was only for Jessica herself. Not for anyone else. So why bother?

Diana had changed all that. She spoke to Jessica with kindness but with fierce honesty too.

'Live your life,' she'd said on their last session, the one before Jessica had flown out to Corfu.

In her pretty room in Hotel Athena, Jessica took the filter-coffee container from her cup and threw it in the bin. Then she smelled the rich, strong coffee it had left behind in the cup. This coffee, like the whole holiday, was her way of trying to live again. It was an experiment. Every day for the past ten days, she'd had a cup of lovely filter coffee when she woke up. She'd packed enough for the whole holiday.

When Jack was alive, they had both loved decent coffee. She enjoyed finding new brands for them to try. She'd bought coffee on the internet for him and had beamed with delight to see him open the package from the postman.

After twenty-seven years of marriage, it was easy to fall out of love with your spouse. But that had never happened to Jessica and Jack.

Three years ago, they'd been thinking fondly of what they might do for their summer holi-days, but then Jack began to feel unwell.

'A cruise,' Jack had said bravely, the day when he went into hospital for the tests.

'A cruise is for old people,' Jessica had joked back, trying to be just as brave. She laid clean pyjamas on his narrow hospital bed. She'd packed another pair, just in case. 'We're not old. Perhaps we should try one of those 18–30 holidays,' she'd added jokily.

Jack's laugh had been loud and genuine. 'And have you in the wet T-shirt contest? Not likely. I'm too old to fight off all the lads who'd want you.'

Jessica loved the idea that Jack still believed anyone would fight over the sight of her in a wet T-shirt contest. With two grown-up sons and the full-figured body of a fifty-three-year-old woman, she was no longer wet T-shirt material. But darling Jack still thought she was. That was love.

There had been no more holidays for them. Jack had died three months later. When Jessica found advertisements for cruises in newspapers now, she felt the nausea rise up in her.

The trip to the Hotel Athena in Corfu was the first time she'd been away since Jack had died. It was another experiment, like the coffee and having a nice glass of wine with dinner. It was an experiment in living. She'd come up with the idea to show Diana that she could live life, really she could. And it was proving lovely.

She took her coffee out on to the balcony and sat on the white cast-iron chair that faced the sea. There were four balconies on that side of the small hotel. On the furthest one, Jessica could see Claire, the quiet fair-haired woman who was married to that tall, handsome man.

Jessica had spoken to Claire and her husband, Anthony, but not much. She hadn't wanted to appear stand-offish, but she didn't really want to talk to people. It was too painful. Seeing Claire and her husband, always holding hands and looking at each other, hurt. It was a reminder of all Jessica had lost.

She'd heard the hotel landlady, Sarah, discussing giving them the honeymoon suite when everyone had arrived. Instantly, Jessica had thought of her own honeymoon with Jack. They'd been totally broke and she'd been pregnant with Marty. Her mother had been tight-lipped at the small wedding ceremony. She'd overheard one of her aunts talking about how awful it was that they 'had to get married'.

Jessica had felt furious. There was no 'had to' about it. She and Jack had been in love. Her being pregnant was icing on the cake.

It had been a great relief to leave the reception and drive at high speed to the small hotel in Wicklow where they were to spend the weekend. Honeymoons weren't so grand then. Not like the big holidays brides had now.

Sometimes, people who'd skimped on their honeymoon made up for it with big holidays for important anniversaries. Like a thirtieth anniversary. Jessica and Jack's thirtieth anniversary would have been in September, two months away.

Jessica took another sip of her coffee and focused on the glittering water of the ocean. She didn't cry much any more. Perhaps human beings were born with so many tears and, once they were all gone, there were no more. She'd finished her supply long ago. Now, she might feel a certain wetness on her lashes, but that was all. She had no crying left in her.

There were so many anniversaries, after Jack had died. The first Christmas, the first birthday, the first anniversary of their wedding . . . that was all supposed to be horrendous, but everyone said it would get better afterwards. Except that it hadn't. The second Christmas had been even worse.

Liam and Marty had been there for the first Christmas after their father died. Liam had come home from Australia and had brought Kathleen, a beautiful Australian girlfriend with a sweet smile, who'd been an angel. Having a non-family member around had helped so much. Marty had come from Cork with his two deranged rescue dogs, and they'd helped too. One dog was a bit like a wolf and liked to make dens with stolen cushions under couches and tables. The other dog was a Labrador type who was hungry all the time and stole food off plates when people weren't looking.

The dogs made people laugh a lot. And when Jessica, Liam and Marty got sad, Kathleen was wise enough to know how to cheer them up. It had been a very different type of Christmas to the ones they were used to, but somehow, they'd got over it.

But last Christmas, the second one without Jack, had been horrible. Liam couldn't afford to fly home from Australia, and Marty, who had just qualified as a vet, had to work over the holidays. Jessica's neat four-bedroomed house felt like a giant empty mansion. The television served up a diet of happy people, merry films and wonderful Christmas routines. So Jessica switched the TV off and tried to read a book about a serial killer in a small American town. The suffering in the novel was a relief after all the enforced Christmas happiness. But she couldn't even concentrate on reading.

She wished there was a naughty dog to steal food from her plate. She almost wished a burglar might try to break in, just so she would have someone to talk to.

She found herself daydreaming about it. The burglar would be young and Jessica would talk him out of his life of crime. And then she realised she couldn't talk anyone out of anything. She was nothing but a crazy widow-woman, she decided. Fifty-five-years-old and going slowly mad. Any sensible burglar would take one look at her and leave. She hadn't been to the hairdresser's in months. When Jack had been alive, she had a shiny brown rinse put in her hair. Now, she had nothing put in. Her hair was shoulder length and mousy grey. She never wore make-up any more and without mascara, her eyelashes were pale.

On her last birthday, the second one since Jack had died, she stayed in bed all day. Her sons had phoned and she'd lied to them.

'Yes, I'm going out to lunch with Lizzie,' she'd said. Lizzie was her best friend and had asked her out to lunch. But Jessica had said no, and Lizzie had given up. She'd asked Jessica out to so many things and Jessica always said no. There was only so much a friend could do, short of dragging her out.

Jessica didn't feel guilty about lying to her sons. It was better to lie and make the boys think she was fine. Would it help if Liam and Marty knew she was wrapped in her duvet, crying? No. They'd worry. They didn't deserve to worry. They were young men with their lives ahead of them. It would be wrong to let them know that their mother's life was over.

On the second wedding anniversary without Jack – it would have been their twenty-ninth wedding anniversary – Jessica got out of bed and went to the shops on her own. She even had a cup of coffee in the cafe beside the supermarket. This was progress, she felt. She didn't have any cake, though. Cake would have felt like celebrating, and Jessica had nothing to celebrate.

On Jack's second birthday since his death – he would have been fifty-eight – Jessica went for a walk on the pier near her home.

What astonished her was that everyone else looked so normal. People laughed. Small dogs still ran madly after seagulls. The seagulls still appeared to taunt the dogs. Mothers pushed huge pushchairs and toddlers still roared to get out of the pushchairs. Once they were out, they yelled to get back in.

Life was going on. Jessica felt huge rage against the whole world for enjoying itself. Didn't they see? Her life was over because her beloved Jack was gone. How could life continue? There simply was no life without Jack.

She had started to cry and she could barely see as she rushed back along the pier to her car. It was Jack's old car. Soon, it would be an antique, Marty joked. They'd never had much money. Jack had been a carpenter and they'd always had food on the table, but there hadn't been money for luxuries.

At home, she sat in front of the big family picture taken the day Marty had got his place in veterinary college. It was hard to remember such happiness. They'd been in the garden beside the old apple tree. Jack loved the garden. They'd bought the old council house he'd grown up in and his father had planted the tree when he was a kid. The family had grown vegetables. Jack's pride and joy were his raspberries. For such a gentle man, he'd waged a fierce war against the birds to stop them stealing his precious fruit.

Sarah and Stavros grew fruit alongside flowers in the garden at the back of the hotel. Jessica had wandered there one day and had found Sarah on her knees weeding a flower bed that was set in a sunny area between the lemon trees.

'This,' said Sarah, pulling on a wild green stalk, 'is like a virus. Once it gets in, you can't control it. It destroys flowers and vegetables.'

'The soil seems hard,' Jessica said, for want of something else to say.

'When I came here first, I couldn't believe how hard it was to grow things. It's tricky when you're always thinking of how to water everything,' Sarah went on. 'So different from home.'

Jessica sat on a cracked stone bench under the nearest lemon tree. 'How long have you lived in Corfu?' she asked.

'Thirty years. Can you believe it?' Sarah wiped her hands on the apron around her comfortable waist. 'It's home to me now.'

'Did you stay because you fell in love with Stavros?' Jessica couldn't believe she'd just asked such a personal question. She rarely spoke to people any more: clearly she'd lost the ability to have normal conversations. 'Sorry,' she said quickly. 'That was very personal . . .'

'No, I prefer that. I hate those "pleased to meet you, isn't the weather lovely?" talks,' said Sarah, smiling. 'Life's too short to waste on such rubbish. Stavros came back to England with me, but he never settled. Norfolk is very pretty but it wasn't Greece. His heart wasn't in it, although he'd have stayed for me.'

She paused and bent to pull up another bit of weed.

'What happened then?'

'His mother became ill and we came back here to run her hotel. At the time, I was afraid I was making the biggest mistake of my life, but now look at me: I love it. You never quite know what's around the corner, do you?' Her shrewd gaze seemed to look into Jessica's very soul.

For the first time in a long time, Jessica didn't feel annoyed at another human being stepping into her mental space. Sarah was a bit like Diana, the counsellor: both women were interested in helping, rather than interested in watching a widow fall apart.

'You don't know what's around the corner,' Jessica said. 'You hope it's a winning lottery ticket, but sometimes, it's a ten-ton truck.'

She began to laugh in astonishment. She'd made a joke. She simply hadn't joked since Jack died.

'What if it's the ten-ton truck of your dreams?' Sarah said, going along with the joke.

'That's the key,' Jessica said.

Sarah sat heavily down on the stone bench beside her. 'Stavros says I shouldn't get on my knees to weed,' she said. 'It's my arthritis. But I like it, it's peaceful.'

'I liked to weed too,' Jessica began, and she started to tell Sarah the whole story.

Since that time, talking to Sarah in the garden behind the hotel, she'd felt very happy in Hotel Athena. She'd found peace there. The question was whether she'd find peace when she flew home.

She'd cross that bridge when she came to it. One more day, Jessica decided, and she'd know what to do.

# Chapter Three

Chloe and Susie woke up at exactly the same time on the last day of their holiday because someone started singing outside their door.

'What?' groaned Chloe, her head appearing out of the nest of sheets for a moment.

'Singing,' said Susie, puzzled.

'Why?'

'Dunno.'

'Shut up,' croaked Chloe at the person who was singing.

Susie tried to sleep again but it was no good. Once she was awake, she was awake. She lay in her cosy single bed in Hotel Athena and worried.

It was all Chloe's fault.

'Let me look after the booking,' she'd said confidently two months before.

Susie should have known better. Chloe had been the one in charge of the Metro in Paris and they'd spent three hours getting lost one day. Three whole hours. But Chloe was one of those people who *sounded* as if they knew what they were doing. In the office – Reilly Insurance – she was very convincing at it.

The supervisor in charge of the Motor Department believed every word Chloe said. Even when she said things like: 'I had shellfish last night for supper and I have food poisoning. That's why I'm sick and have to go home.'

Susie and the rest of the staff would be watching open-mouthed at Chloe's performance. Surely nobody would believe such outright fibs? Any idiot could see that Chloe was suffering from having had too many tequilas after the football match the night before. But no, Chloe would be believed and would get sent home.

They'd been friends for four years. Four years in various departments in Reilly Insurance, and now they were climbing the ladder in Motor. They were twenty-seven. They had nice clothes, several designer handbags apiece, and rented a lovely mews apartment together. They knew each other's families. Chloe had been to Susie's home in Galway many times, and Susie had visited Chloe's mother's house in Cork. They took care of each other and vetted each other's boyfriends. They went on diets together. WeightWatchers was the best. They shared a pair of roomy black jeans for fat days. Size fourteen. They were both twelves now, but you never knew. It was a good idea to have a back-up outfit for emergencies.

Hotel Athena was lovely, Susie knew. Sweet,

really. If she'd been here with Finn, she'd have loved it. They could have had a room with a double bed. They might never have got out of the bed.

But as a holiday for two single girls wanting to have fun, it was a total disaster.

It was a simple mistake, Chloe kept saying.

Hotel Athena was on page 45 of the brochure. Hotel Athenee was on page 47. Hotel Athenee was close to nightlife, tavernas, etc. It had a disco, three pools and offered a huge range of excursions. The photo in the brochure showed a Greek boat loaded with tanned, gorgeous men and women dancing in the sun. They were holding up wine glasses and smiling. You could almost hear the music blaring out of the boat's speakers. They looked like people in a Coca Cola advertisement. *That* was the sort of holiday Susie wanted. She wanted to be a skinny, tanned blonde in shades.

Well, she'd need to lose a few pounds first. But she was blonde and, after two weeks here, she was tanned. Except that Hotel Athenee was on the other side of the island, along with all the crazy nightlife. Hotel Athena was a quiet family hotel in a family resort. The most exciting thing that happened here was that the banana boat occasionally started to sink a bit under the weight and a few twelve-year-olds squealed as they fell in the sea.

There were no crazy disco bars, no places with karaoke machines where Chloe could launch into Tina Turner's 'Nutbush City Limits', her mother's favourite song. Not that she could sing or anything, but she could dance like Tina and if she backcombed her hair, it stood up like Tina's wig.

There were no gorgeous single men to look at. There was one fabulous-looking guy, Anthony Reynolds. He was very like Ashton Kutcher, but older, obviously. He was here with his wife and he never so much as looked at Susie or Chloe. Not that they wanted a married guy, but still. It would have been nice to have someone admire them. Chloe, who was between men, wanted some eye-candy for her holiday.

Even Susie, who had her darling fiancé, Finn, waiting at home, never objected to having a nice guy admire her. It was daft, she knew, but it always made her feel less self-conscious if she caught an admiring gaze. It was proof that the diet had been a success and that she didn't look too pale in her bikini.

The first day they'd arrived, they'd been exhausted and happy to lie on the beach with plans to check out the resort that night. At nine p.m., they'd arrived downstairs in the hotel, all glammed up. Susie was wearing her fringed purple T-shirt dress. She'd curled her blonde hair with her GHD irons and she'd lined her eyes with lots of silvery grey liner. Chloe, who'd had a spray tan before she left Ireland, was wearing tight white jeans and a sparkly camisole. They looked fabulous.

The man on the desk in the hotel stared at them when they asked where the nightlife was.

'Nightlife?' he repeated.

He was married to the woman who'd welcomed them, Susie realised. Stavros, that was his name.

'Yeah, pubs, clubs, bars,' she said, smiling. Old people were a gas, weren't they? He probably thought this was late. But it was early. Early if you were twenty-seven years old.

'Bars,' Stavros said, finally understanding. 'The Kourous, run by a friend of mine, is down the street. To the left.' He helpfully led them to the door and pointed them in the right direction. 'There are many restaurants there, too. Anna's is the place with the red lamps. She is my cousin and a wonderful cook. You must try her dolmades. Wonderful,' he said, kissing his fingers. 'And the baklava. All women love it.'

Baklava. Great – must be a cocktail, Susie thought.

Baklava was dessert, layers of filo pastry, honey and nuts. Stavros was right: they did love it. It was the most exciting thing about the whole night. The resort was pretty and the dolmades in Anna's restaurant were marvellous. But the people in the resort were all families or couples. The place was dedicated to families and children. There were no lively bars, no live music. Apart from those three mad old fellas with strange Greek instruments who played music in the restaurant.

'Dance, ladies, dance!' they urged Chloe and Susie. Even the three mad fellas could see that girls like Susie and Chloe were not made for sitting down in restaurants.

'Do you know any Lady GaGa?' Chloe asked them.

'Gaga? We are all gaga!' the oldest of them laughed.

The next morning, the holiday company rep did her best to help them out. She was a sturdy Kerry girl called Maire and she was used to dealing with anxious holidaymakers. The week before, she'd dealt with a man who'd broken his ankle trying to show his wife that you *could* climb from the ground up to their second-floor balcony. 'Any time there's nobody actually in hospital in a cast getting a morphine painkiller inserted, I don't worry about it too much,' Maire said sensibly.

'I can see how it went wrong,' she agreed, once she'd heard their explanation about the hotel mix-up. They were all sitting on the veranda in Hotel Athena, sipping juice.

'My fault,' said Chloe, for about the tenth time that morning. 'I'm sorry, Susie. Really sorry.'

Maire let them flick through the brochure. It was torture. Susie could see all the other fabulous hotels they could have gone to. Ones with discos in the hotel itself, ones with pictures of people partying. Corfu, as it said in the brochure, had something for everybody.

'I'll make some phone calls,' Maire promised. 'See what I can do. I can't promise anything, though. It's not really our fault, you see. The hotel's lovely, there's nothing wrong with it. Everyone who comes here wants to come back, actually, which isn't always the case. Sarah and Stavros are marvellous people, but I'll check it out and see if we can get you somewhere else.'

By late afternoon, Maire was back with the terrible news that there was nowhere else. It was peak season. All the other hotels were full, and unless the girls paid for two weeks somewhere else, they would have to stay in the Hotel Athena.

'I'm sorry, I really tried to call in some favours,' Maire said. 'This isn't your sort of place, but unless you get taxis every night to other resorts, you're stuck.'

Susie and Chloe had no money for taxis every night. Maybe once or twice, but that was it. The whole point of going to a resort was that they wouldn't have to worry about transport.

Four days after they arrived, they booked a taxi with the hotel and went ten miles to the next resort. After the quiet of the Hotel Athena, the noise was a shock. The place throbbed with action. The streets were full of girls dressed like themselves. Loud music blared from bars, and men eyed them up. Handsome men and girls stood on the streets beckoning them into bars. It was heaven.

Even the hangover the next day hadn't been too bad. They'd lain on the beach and talked about how much fun it had been. They'd made friends with a gang from Chester and they were all going to meet up again in two days. In Club Paradise. Susie had loved Club Paradise. It was where she'd met Lucas.

And then . . . Susie had to get out of bed. The person singing outside their room was the cleaner, she realised. The Hotel Athena was spotless, but the cleaners started at about seven in the morning, which was when all the families got up.

Normally, she pulled a pillow over her head to smother the noise of the cleaners and the kids. Now, she knew she wouldn't get back to sleep. She was too worried and she couldn't bear the anxious feeling that came over her when she thought about this. She'd have a fag. They'd bought four hundred in duty-free on the plane over and they were nearly all gone, with just one day of the holiday left.

'I bet you'll go back on the fags,' Finn had said before she left. 'Chloe's still smoking, you will too.'

'Honestly, what do you think I am?' Susie had demanded.

Susie's fingers shook as she lit her cigarette. Finn. Oh hell, Finn. Her fiancé.

She and Finn had set the date for the wedding. It was to be held the following year, in the long summer holidays. Just twelve months away. They'd had none of the trauma other couples had over choosing a venue for the reception. Finn's mother insisted it be held in their garden. In a marquee.

Susie's mother had gone white when she heard this. 'In their garden, in a marquee,' she'd repeated, as if she hadn't heard it right.

'I know,' groaned Susie.

Her family home in Galway was a three-bedroom semi. Her father used to joke that the back garden was so small, he could cut the grass with his electric razor. He was a great practical joker and once, when her mother had been sick, he'd cheered her up by pretending to do just that.

'How big is their garden, then?' Susie's mother had asked.

Susie wasn't sure how to answer without upsetting her mother. She thought back to the first time she'd seen Finn's house. It was huge, a big grey house set on four acres. It had stables, a herb garden, and there had once been an outdoor swimming pool, but it had been turned into a sunken garden. Finn's mother, Gloria, had shown her proudly around the house.

'The servants used these stairs, years ago,' Gloria had said, pointing out a tiny, steep staircase beside the kitchen. Susie didn't like Finn's mother much. She felt that Gloria returned the favour. In fact, Susie was sure that Gloria thought she was common. An insurance clerk from Galway wasn't suitable for her darling boy, even if they worked in the same company. Finn worked in management.

Finn couldn't see it. 'She loves you, you mad

thing,' he said. 'Mum is just a bit formal until she gets to know you. Her father worked in the diplomatic service, you know. She was brought up in a different world.'

Gloria mentioned the diplomatic service all the time. She'd gone to posh parties in embassies all around the world wherever her father was posted. This was where she'd learned to do things 'the right way'. She was very keen on things being 'the right way' at Finn and Susie's wedding. Susie felt guilty that Finn's parents were shouldering most of the cost of the reception. So she kept quiet.

Susie's dad liked the idea of a bit of lamb at the reception.

'Lamb and spuds,' he said. 'That'll do for my dinner. And mushroom soup for starters.'

Susie couldn't tell him that Gloria had her heart set on scallops on a bed of risotto, followed by peach sorbet and then beef wellington.

'To be different from the herd, how about a wedding cake made entirely of profiteroles?' Gloria had said.

Susie had to look up beef wellington on the Internet.

Unfortunately, she'd also looked up a holiday diet. This was where things had started to go wrong. She and Chloe called it the Severe Holiday Diet. It consisted of diet breakfast cereal and one slimming supplement drink for dinner. She and Chloe had done that for three whole days before they'd gone away. They'd lost pounds. Susie had felt weak on the airport bus, but it was worth it. Except that her engagement ring had been loose on her finger. A single sapphire with four tiny diamonds at each corner.

'If you lose it, imagine –' Chloe had said as they flew out to Corfu.

Susie had put it on her middle finger.

'Now you don't look engaged,' Chloe said.

'It hardly matters,' Susie pointed out. 'I know I'm engaged.'

If she'd been wearing her engagement ring on the correct finger, Lucas would have seen it. Or someone would have seen it and said, 'You're engaged.'

A line would have been drawn in the sand. Men – Lucas – would have realised she had a fiancé. He wouldn't have gazed deeply into her eyes. Nothing would have happened. Except it had.

# Chapter Four

Claire put the last of her belongings into the suitcase and zipped it up. She loved those articles in magazines about how to pack your perfect holiday wardrobe, but she forgot all the advice as soon as she started. One pair of flat shoes and one pair of heels was never enough. The high heels that went with her silky blue skirt looked ridiculous with her floral dress. So she'd need a separate pair of heels, like her wedge sandals. And the silvery flip-flops, just in case. Despite the trouble she took, she still never took the right stuff.

At least today, hours before the coach came to take them to the airport, it wasn't too difficult. All she had to do was squash everything she'd brought back into the suitcase.

She found herself remembering a back-packing holiday she'd been on years ago, when she hadn't brought enough stuff. Determined not to pack too much, she'd packed too little. She'd taken flimsy T-shirts that were perfect for the beach, but she forgot to bring a fleece for travelling or earplugs or socks or her phone charger.

It had been the most amazing holiday, though. She and Anthony had gone with the gang they'd grown up with in Bray. Their parents had all moved into a new housing estate just outside Dublin in the 1970s and their kids had made friends. There were ten of them and they'd stayed friends through different schools, through jobs and college, through everything.

There had always been something between Claire Flynn and Anthony Reynolds.

They'd been totally different. He was a rebel, wore black leather jackets and roared around on a motorbike. Claire was a responsible student, studied hard and never gave her parents a moment's worry.

She'd got top marks in her state school exams. Anthony had actually missed one of the exams after a wild night out. His best subject was art, but he refused to study art history, insisting that the exam should be about painting. He was absolutely not the sort of person she should have fancied, but she did. It wasn't just that he was gorgeous. It was the distant sadness in his eyes that drew her in. When she'd got a place in a teacher-training college, she knew she'd hardly see Anthony or the gang much any more. The college was on the other side of the city.

She'd either be in college or travelling to and from it.

And then Anthony appeared at the college one Friday evening, on his motorbike with a spare helmet. In his leathers, with his tanned skin and unruly hair, he looked sexy and dangerous. The other students looked at him enviously.

'You came to drive me home?' Claire said that first time, astonished and touched. On the bike, they'd be home in no time. Normally it took her two hours on buses and trains. It was the kindest thing anyone had ever done for her.

'I got off work early,' he said. He was apprenticed with a local mechanic. 'And I thought of you trailing across the city for hours. I don't know if you like the bike, though.'

Claire's eyes shone. 'I love the bike,' she said, even though she'd never been on one in her life.

From then on, they were a couple. A very mismatched couple, according to most people. Claire understood why people thought it would never last. Anthony looked as if he should be dating a kohl-eyed blonde with a leather jacket and spray-on jeans. Claire was freckly, with fair curly hair, and people often called her 'cute', which she hated. Her only claim to beauty was her eyes, which were cornflower blue and luminous. Spray-on jeans looked stupid on her.

But she loved Anthony with her heart and soul, and it seemed as if he loved her back. When she got her first teaching job, they bought a small house together not far from where their parents lived. They married the following year and it was nearly the happiest day of Claire's life. Anthony's older brother, Stevie, insisted the wedding party take advantage of the hotel's residents' bar. In the end, Claire spent a lot of her first night as a married woman waiting for her husband to come up to the bridal suite. He was badly hung over the next day and kept throwing up on the flight to Alicante.

'I'm so sorry, love, please don't hate me,' he'd begged that night as Claire tucked him up in bed to let him sleep. She was going downstairs to have dinner in the hotel dining room alone. 'I don't hate you, you big idiot,' she said affectionately.

Anthony's drinking took on a pattern. He seemed to be in control ninety per cent of the time, able to go out with friends and have a few glasses of wine and nothing else. Those times, Claire felt utterly happy: he didn't have an alcohol problem, she told herself. He was fine. And then a night would come when it seemed as if Anthony had decided to get drunk.

When he did, his dark eyes looked sadder than ever. Claire would watch him drinking and wish she could fix that dark place inside him. The darkness was what made him drink, she was sure. Whatever the sadness was, she never seemed to be able to help.

Jessica laid out her souvenir presents on the hotel bed and worked out who would get what. The hand-painted plates would be lovely for her friend, Lizzie. They'd be a sort of apology too. Lizzie had tried to get Jessica to go on holidays with her many times since Jack had died, and Jessica had said no every time. And then she'd upped and gone on holiday on her own after a few sessions with a grief counsellor. Lizzie was a good friend.

The bronzed horse statues would be great for Marty, although very heavy to transport. Liam and his girlfriend, Kathleen, would like the Greek scrolls. They'd be easy to post to Australia, too.

She'd got a pretty hand-painted vase for Diana, although she wasn't sure if you were allowed to buy a counsellor presents. Possibly not.

Looking at her few gifts on the bed, Jessica realised that her world had shrunk. Once, she would have bought so many more presents. A trinket for the neighbours on each side, something for Jack's older brother, Tommy, who loved getting things from abroad. He adored snow globes. Jack and Jessica had had so much fun over the years, trying to buy snow globes everywhere they went. The more colourful they were, the more Tommy loved them.

She hadn't known how lucky she was then, Jessica decided. She'd always been worried about the future. Would they have enough money? Would the boys do well in school or college?

Jack wasn't a worrier. 'What will be, will be,' he used to say.

If anyone else had said it, Jessica might have wanted to hit them. But Jack could say it and make it sound like words from the Bible. He had that sort of way with him.

He was calm and wise.

But Jessica had worried in spite of her husband. And she'd wasted time worrying when she should have been enjoying life.

In her litany of worries, she'd never thought of Jack dying of cancer when he was still a young man. All those years of worrying, and it turned out that she'd worried about the wrong things.

\* \* \*

40

Susie shook her zebra-print bikini on the balcony to get the sand out of it. It was from Top Shop, like something Kate Moss might wear. She could imagine the pictures in the magazines: Kate, all tanned and leggy, with a straw hat and gladiator sandals, getting off a yacht in St. Tropez. A zebra bikini needed jewellery, and Susie had brought along a couple of cheap gold necklaces with dangling stones, one amber and one pink. She'd worn the whole lot on the third day of the holiday, when everything had still been fine.

Just herself and Chloe, two girls having fun and ready to enjoy themselves. They'd been so upset about the Hotel Athena, but it had been hard to remain upset for long. The hotel itself was too lovely, the sun was too hot and the sky was too gloriously blue. The water down at the beach was like the water in postcards.

Susie used to think that photographers faked that type of water. She'd grown up in Galway and was used to the fierce waves of the Atlantic. She loved the wild beauty of the sea there. But it was never like the sea in Greece, a deep, calm blue that lapped gently against the beach.

If only it was that day again, the day she'd worn the zebra bikini for the first time.

Susie closed her eyes and wished with all her

heart that she could turn back time. Back to the time before Lucas.

The first night in Club Paradise, she'd only met him briefly. She and Chloe had made friends with the girls from Chester, most of whom worked in an insurance call centre.

'Like us!' squealed Chloe, delighted. Her delight was partly fuelled by two enormous vodkas with Red Bull. The barmen didn't measure drinks, they kept pouring until you said stop.

The life and soul of the Chester gang was a tall girl named Shireen, who was ready for everything, including having a go at the limbo-dancing competition on the beach.

Lucas had arrived later. His cousin was one of the Chester girls and he was with a group of guys who worked in Bristol. For several hours, they all danced together and laughed. Susie couldn't keep her eyes off Lucas, but he didn't talk. He didn't dance either. When Susie danced, she was aware of his eyes on her.

It wasn't disloyal to Finn, she decided. It was OK to have other guys admire her. Then she realised her engagement ring was on the wrong finger. She hadn't said she was engaged. She would next time.

When Susie and Chloe finally got a taxi home at three in the morning, they promised to come back in a few nights. Plans were made and phone numbers were exchanged.

Chloe fell asleep in the taxi on the way back to the Hotel Athena, but Susie didn't sleep. She was thinking about Lucas and how special it would be if someone like Lucas fancied you. He was incredibly good-looking but didn't seem to be aware of all the women looking at him. That was nice. Susie hated vain men on principle.

The taxi lurched to a halt outside the hotel and she pulled a sleepy Chloe inside. Back in their hotel room, Chloe fell on to her bed fully dressed and was asleep instantly. Susie took off her friend's strappy sandals and pulled off her skirt. She tried to take off Chloe's long dangly earrings, but it was impossible. Instead, she pulled the duvet up and left her.

In the cool of their pretty room, the memory of Club Paradise and Lucas was already fading. Susie couldn't quite believe she'd spent the evening looking at him. She was engaged, for heaven's sake.

Before she got into her cosy bed in the Hotel Athena, Susie kissed the little photo of Finn that she kept on the locker between the beds. It was a wonderful picture and showed off Finn's incredible smile and the wild red of his spiky hair. Finn wasn't exactly handsome. Women didn't watch him as he walked past. In the sun, his back looked like a join-the-dots puzzle with freckles. But he was the kindest, warmest, funniest man she'd ever met. It was a mystery how a woman like Gloria could have produced such a son.

The second night in Club Paradise, Lucas and his friends were there from the beginning. Susie was shocked at how much she wanted to talk to him. Lucas was different from his friends. They were all good-looking, confident and wore cool clothes. But Lucas was quieter. He sat there watching everyone from narrow grey eyes hidden behind shaggy tawny hair. He was very brown with defined muscles in his arms, like someone who worked out a lot. Susie watched him idly twirling the leather bracelets on his wrist.

His friend was chatty, so she talked to him instead.

'What do you all do?' she asked, idly.

'I work in a bank,' the guy said gloomily. 'It's no fun, trust me. Lucas used to work in an estate agents, but that's all over now.'

'I write songs,' Lucas said suddenly, looking straight at Susie.

44

'Wow,' said Susie. Then felt stupid for just saying 'wow'. She'd sounded like an idiot. 'I mean, that's amazing, not many people can do that . . .' She was babbling now.

At that exact moment, Shireen said they should buy some beer and head to the beach. 'Let's swim . . . No.' Shireen's eyes gleamed in the club's lights. 'Let's skinny-dip.'

Susie's mother had warned her about the sea and alcohol.

'Never swim when you've had a drink, promise me?' she'd said.

'Mum, I'm twenty-seven, what sort of ninny do you think I am?' Susie had said. 'I'd never do anything that daft.'

Lucas got to his feet and held a hand out to Susie. She got up from her seat so fast that she knocked over her nearly full cocktail glass.

Lots of other people had clearly had the same idea, as the beach was busy with groups of people sitting on the sand, laughing and drinking. It was much quieter here, away from the noise of the bars, although the thump of bass music could be heard. It felt amazing to be outside at night with a warm breeze wrapping itself around her.

Susie and Lucas walked hand in hand. He held the hand with the engagement ring on it, but the ring was on the wrong finger. Would it have made a difference if it had been on the right finger? Susie didn't know. But under the silver Greek moon, it made perfect sense to walk hand in hand with this man she barely knew. He held her left hand. Her engagement ring felt different on the wrong finger. Susie knew she should tell Lucas she was engaged, but somehow, she didn't know how. He'd think she was a tart if she told him now. Engaged and flirting with someone else.

Nothing would happen anyway, she decided. So it didn't matter.

Chloe had teamed up with another of Lucas' friends, who was called Troy and was teased endlessly about it.

'Are you Helen? Helen of Troy, gettit?' giggled someone. 'The face that launched a thousand ships.'

'Wasn't Brad Pitt in that film? He's gorgeous.'

Chloe grinned and ignored them all. But she did shoot Susie a firm glare at one point. The glare said, 'You're engaged! What are you *doing*?'

Susie couldn't help herself. It was as if she was being bewitched, in the way the Ancient Greek sailors had been bewitched by long-haired sirens and led on to dangerous rocks.

With the waves lapping on to the shore, Lucas and Susie kissed and held each other. It was like being in a film. She didn't feel like herself. She was someone else, someone exciting, kissing a mysterious man on a beach.

'I share a room with three of the guys,' Lucas said. 'We can't go there. Your place?'

'It's miles away,' she replied. Again, she wished she and Chloe were staying close to Club Paradise instead of in the sedate Hotel Athena.

It was nearly dawn when Susie and Chloe got a taxi back to their hotel. Susie's face felt raw from kissing.

Once again, Chloe fell asleep in the taxi. Susie envied her friend her ability to fall asleep so easily.

This time, Susie had felt even more guilty when she got back to their hotel. Chloe was right – what *had* she been doing?

All the next day, when they lay on the beach after getting up at one o'clock, she felt guilty.

'Are you hung over?' Chloe asked.

Susie wasn't. She hadn't drunk that much, she wasn't much of a drinker. If she had a hangover, it was a guilt one. What had come over her on the beach? She'd never cheated on Finn before. She wasn't that sort of girl.

At least she would never see Lucas again.

And then that evening, Lucas had simply arrived. She and Chloe had been sitting on the veranda after dinner in the hotel and he'd appeared. He was as gorgeous as ever.

Again, Chloe didn't say anything. But her eyes still said, 'Are you mad?'

Sarah, the hotel owner, had chatted politely with him and brought him out a glass of wine.

When Lucas and Susie walked along the beach hand in hand, she knew where they'd end up. Chloe didn't come back to the blue and white hotel bedroom until midnight, when Lucas and Susie were lying naked in the single bed.

'Is three a crowd?' Chloe asked awkwardly.

Lucas said, 'Yes.'

He dressed quickly in the bathroom, kissed Susie goodbye and left.

Susie snuggled down in her bed and dreamed of a Brad Pitt-style movie where a handsome man just like Lucas rescued her from evil. It was a glorious dream, the sort of dream a person doesn't want to wake up from. In it, Susie was beautiful in a way she wasn't in real life. All men adored her and wanted her. But only Lucas could have her, his lean body melting into hers . . .

Then she woke up and into a nightmare.

Chloe was snoring in her bed and the sun was streaming into the room through a chink in the curtains. Finn's photo on the bedside locker seemed to be staring right at her, saying, 'What have you done?'

The craziness that had come over her every time she'd seen Lucas had gone. To be replaced by a black hole of guilt.

What had she done? She'd ruined everything.

'Do I have to put things like shampoo in two plastic bags?' demanded Chloe from inside the room.

Susie gave her zebra bikini one last shake.

'Unless you want shampoo to spill all over your clothes, I would,' she said in a resigned voice. It was time to go home to the rest of her life with this big lie hanging over her. The lie about Lucas.

# Chapter Five

'You're thinking about Lucas again, aren't you?' asked Chloe.

They'd just got on to the plane and were sitting in a middle and a window seat.

'No,' Susie said, 'I'm not thinking about Lucas.' She was thinking about darling Finn and how she'd betrayed him.

'You are. I can tell,' Chloe insisted. 'Listen, Susie, there's no point telling Finn what happened. What would that achieve?'

Chloe's point, delivered every day since Susie had slept with Lucas, was that Finn should never know. 'What a person doesn't know, can't hurt them,' Susie said wisely.

It did sound wise. But it also sounded wrong somehow to Susie. She and Finn were going to be married and surely the whole point of that was honesty? Why get married if you had loads of secrets?

But the time for telling had passed. Finn phoned often. He phoned on his way to work the morning after Susie had slept with Lucas.

'Hello, fiancée,' he'd said. 'How are you? I miss you.'

Susie didn't think it was possible to feel more guilty than she already did. But hearing Finn say that he missed her moved the guilt up a level. She hated herself at that moment. How had she betrayed lovely Finn for a few moments with Lucas? What sort of a terrible person was she?

It had been a crazy holiday game, she realised. Lucas was the most gorgeous guy around and he'd liked her. Her self-esteem had soared. Instead of leaving it at that, she'd gone further. She'd wanted to prove that he really fancied her, that she wasn't a nobody from Galway as Finn's mother seemed to think.

Chloe settled her duty-free purchases under her seat and picked up the flight magazine to see what else she could buy. Chloe's credit card was nearly always stretched to its limit. That was another difference between them, Susie realised. Chloe was a great believer in worrying about things tomorrow: credit-card bills, holiday flings. It would all work out somehow, was her motto.

Sitting in the window seat, her heart heavy, Susie realised she was very different. But she could see no way out of this dilemma except to follow Chloe's rules. She couldn't tell Finn about Lucas. He'd be devastated, and then he mightn't marry her. And Susie couldn't bear to think of a life without Finn. Lucas had been a moment of madness, but Finn was the one she loved.

By chance, Tricia, Pat and the children were in the seats beside Claire and Anthony. Tricia sat with the children and Pat sat on the other side of the aisle, with Claire in the middle seat and Anthony at the window. Claire hated sitting near the window. She was a nervous flier and the less she saw of the clouds and the earth far away, the better.

She sat back with her eyes closed and Pat and Anthony chatted over her head. Pat was fascinated to learn that Anthony had a motorbike.

'I've always wanted one, but you can't get one with kid seats,' he joked.

Claire could well imagine Tricia raising her eyes to heaven at this. She could hear her busily settling her daughters for the journey.

'Here's your colouring book and when the plane is high in the sky, I'll put down the table and you can colour,' she was saying brightly. Eyes closed, Claire smiled. Tricia was such a wonderful mother. Perhaps Claire could be that sort of mother, the sort who went everywhere with a big bag of toys for the children to play with. She let herself float off into a fantasy world where she, Anthony and their two beautiful children were on a plane.

Maybe it could be a plane with four seats in the middle so they wouldn't be split up. Anthony would be on one aisle, fastening one of the children's seatbelts. She'd be on the other aisle doing the same thing. Their eyes would meet with love and sheer happiness at being with their family.

Claire rarely allowed herself to play the children fantasy. It was too painful. So many of their friends had kids now. Each time they were told of another pregnancy, Claire felt a little part of herself wither up and die. There was no way she could come off the contraceptive pill to start a family with Anthony the way he was. There could be no joy with a newborn baby with a father who drank himself to oblivion all the time.

'What's really awful is that he's a good man. He'd be such a good father,' her sister, Louisa said. Louisa was the only person in whom Claire confided. Telling people the reality of how much Anthony drank would be like a betrayal of him. So she lied for him. She phoned the garage to say he wouldn't be in that day because he had a virus. She went to parties on her own and said he was working. It was easier to say that than to explain that he was lying in bed with a horrific hangover. Or that he was drunk already, only fit to lie on the couch in a haze.

Louisa knew the truth. That over the past three years, Anthony's drinking had grown steadily worse. During the day, he functioned normally. But he got drunk at all social events and Claire was an expert at getting him out before too many people noticed. He drank at home several times a week after she'd gone to bed.

'Sorry,' he'd murmur when he fell into the bed at midnight and his breath reeked of booze. 'Just a nightcap to help me sleep.'

He was never angry, violent or abusive. He simply couldn't stop drinking until all the alcohol in the house was gone. The next day, he'd be so repentant that she'd forgive him. 'I don't know why I do it,' he'd say, bewildered. Looking into those sad, dark eyes, Claire believed him. If only she could release him from the mysterious pain inside him.

Two months ago, Claire had sobbed down the phone to her sister and told her that Anthony had actually wet their bed the night before. Why this was the last straw, she didn't know. But it was.

'You should leave him,' Louisa said.

'I can't leave him. I love him. What would he do without me?'

'Drink himself into the grave, which is what he's doing now, even though you're still with him,' Louisa answered. 'You can't stop him, Claire. You deserve better. A life, kids, a man who's there for you, not one who's looking for answers in the bottom of a bottle.'

Anthony had come home very drunk that night.

'Just a few beers with the lads from work,' he said lightly.

Claire knew he was lying. The men from work didn't go drinking on Tuesdays. More likely, Anthony had gone into The Coral Reef, a dingy pub near the fire station, and had sunk several double vodkas.

'I'm leaving,' she said. 'I'm sleeping in the spare room tonight. I don't want to wake up in your urine.'

She didn't know what was harder, saying it or watching his face as she said it.

'I can't cope any more, Anthony. I don't want to spend the rest of my life with an alcoholic.'

There, she'd said it. The word they'd never used. Alcoholic. Once said, it could never be taken back.

Anthony had sat with his hands over his face. 'I am so sorry,' he said, and he began to sob helplessly.

Claire's heart ached, but she knew what she had to do.

'Sorry isn't enough. You say that every time it happens, and it still happens again. I can't watch you destroy yourself and I can't fix you. I'm sorry, but it's over, Anthony. I feel like I'm going mad, watching you doing this to you, to us. Your alcoholism is killing us, did you know that?'

He looked up with agony in his eyes. 'I know.'

Instead of feeling relief that she'd used the world alcoholic and he hadn't denied it, she'd felt nothing but pain. She had gone to the spare room, locked the door and phoned Louisa.

'I did it,' she sobbed. 'It was horrible. I don't know if it was the right thing, Louisa. If you could have seen his face. He loves me . . .'

'He loves booze more,' Louisa said. 'Remember that.'

Claire had remembered it the next day as she packed her suitcases and moved into Louisa's spare room. Louisa told everyone what had happened.

'No more covering up for him,' she told her sister. 'Tough love.'

Two weeks later, Anthony turned up on

Louisa's doorstep. He was thin, pale and utterly sober. Louisa grudgingly let him in.

'I haven't had a drink in eight days,' Anthony said to Claire. He held her hands and looked ready to cry. 'I promise I won't drink again. Please, please will you come back?'

'You're mad,' Louisa told her as Claire packed her suitcases to leave with Anthony.

'I can't help it. I love him,' Claire said. 'And he's not drinking any more. Not a drop.'

A month later, they'd booked a last-minute flight to Corfu.

'We need a break and you need sun on your bones,' Claire told Anthony. They didn't talk about it being a new start, but it was. Without the haunting presence of alcohol, they were like newly weds getting used to each other.

Spending time with all their old friends at home was difficult. People still offered Anthony a drink. Nobody considered his feelings when they waved their drinks around. Getting away from it all was the perfect idea. And it had turned out that way. Claire would always remember Hotel Athena with something close to love. It had given her back her husband.

As if he knew she'd been thinking about him, Anthony reached out and put his hand over hers.

'All right, love?' he asked.

'Great,' Claire said, smiling. 'We had a lovely time, didn't we?' she added wistfully.

In reply, Anthony squeezed her hand. 'Best holiday I ever had,' he said.

Claire knew it couldn't have been the easiest holiday for him. It was only a little over two months since he'd stopped drinking. But together, they'd got through it. Because they were together, it had become the best holiday ever.

Jessica had three seats to herself. One of the advantages of travelling alone, she decided. She chose to sit next to the window and put her magazines on the middle seat. On the flight to Corfu, she'd been sitting beside two young men who'd slept most of the flight. It was hard to clamber over them when she'd had to visit the toilet. Now, she could wander at will.

Sarah from Hotel Athena had given her some gardening magazines for the flight.

'There's something very comforting about flicking through them,' Sarah said, handing over a big bundle. 'I get lots sent to me and I reread them.'

'I can't take these,' Jessica protested.

'You'll be back in Corfu. You can return them to me then and bring me new ones,' Sarah said.

Briefly, Jessica felt like a cheat. She didn't

know if she'd be back. Tonight, when she got home, she was going to decide. She wanted to see what the house felt like when she went inside. Would the absolute hopelessness of her life swamp her again? Would being in the house she'd shared with Jack make her feel that there was no point being alive? She wouldn't know until she got home.

In Corfu, the misery that came over her was less powerful. She felt freer, almost happy. Sometimes, when she was walking along the rocks on the beach near the hotel, she forgot about her pain.

In the hills, she'd visited an old monastery Sarah had told her about. Despite all the tourists milling around, it was a sacred place. Jessica let the prayerful atmosphere sink into her soul. She sat on stone steps outside a tiny shrine and thought of all the others, like herself, who'd come here hoping for peace. For the first time in a long while, she didn't feel so alone. Lots of other people had been in pain here. Lots would be again. People still managed to live in spite of the pain.

In her handbag, pushed carefully under the airline seat in front of her, she carried a small icon she'd bought from a shop beside the monastery. It was a classic Greek Orthodox icon, a vision of a glowing saint with kind eyes. It felt comforting to have it close to her.

Pat had a couple of bottles of Greek brandy in a plastic bag under the seat in front of him. They clinked from time to time as Pat banged into them with his feet. Claire had a headache and the clinking noise was really irritating.

Pat was clueless, she decided. He'd had two little bottles of wine with his meal and the scent of wine filled the air. She hoped Anthony couldn't smell it, and then realised that she couldn't protect him from the world. People would always drink. The whole planet wouldn't stop drinking wine or brandy just because he had to. He would have to deal with it.

Jessica bought an Irish newspaper from one of the stewardesses. All the news was gloomy. Redundancies, bankruptcies, cuts in the health service. After briefly flicking through it, she folded it up and left it on the outside seat. Perhaps that's why Corfu had been such an escape, it was so far away from normal life. It had only new memories, no old ones.

Jack used to love reading the newspaper. He read a broadsheet from cover to cover every day and bought two at the weekends. Jessica liked the magazines that came with the Sunday papers. She read about television stars and their lives. She marked off television programmes they could watch. Their tastes in programmes were very different. She loved films and her soaps. Jack had left school at sixteen and loved watching history programmes.

'This is my education,' he'd say whenever Jessica found him glued to another documentary on the History Channel.

'Crazy man,' she'd say lovingly. He might not have gone to college, but he was one of the smartest people she knew.

Jessica had been to secretarial college for a year. She was the first one of her family to have had any third-level education. She remembered how proud she and Jack had been when both their sons went to college. Her own parents had thought that a degree was something for rich people's children. The world was a different place now.

Outside the plane window, the sky was a sullen grey. The blue skies of Greek airspace had been replaced by gloomy clouds. It looked like thunder. Jessica shivered. Being in a plane made her feel very fragile and scared.

'I wish you were here, Jack,' she said silently.

\* \* \*

Chloe had chosen a perfume gift set with six tiny bottles of Calvin Klein scents from the duty-free trolley. She'd opened them all many times and was dabbing them on her wrists.

'I can't decide which one I like most,' she sighed happily. 'Obsession, I think. That's my favourite.'

No matter how much perfume Chloe put on, all Susie could smell was the scent of toasted cheese sandwiches mixed with what had to be a small baby with a dirty nappy. As she did every time she got on a plane, Susie dreamed about having loads of money and being able to fly at the front end of the plane. Dirty nappies and toasted sandwiches probably weren't allowed up there. It was all champagne and people handing you hot towels. And you had your own TV screen on your seat. There was no twisting your head to see the big screen at the top of their part of the plane.

Still, watching a film was better than nothing. She put her headphones on and tried to watch the in-flight movie. Jennifer Aniston was in it. Susie liked Jennifer because she seemed normal.

Susie had been watching only a few minutes when the film was paused and a passenger announcement came on.

'We've been warned about thunderstorms

ahead and there is the risk of turbulence for about ten minutes. The captain has put the "fasten seatbelts" sign on and we'd ask you not to visit the toilets during this time.'

The movie went back on. Turbulence, thought Susie. Great. She wished she'd brought some of those travel-sickness tablets.

The announcement made Jessica feel even more anxious. Jack had told her what turbulence was and had explained that it wasn't at all dangerous. He used to hold her hand during bumpy flights on their holidays. Now, she had no one to hold her hand. She quickly took off her seatbelt, got her handbag, and clicked on the seatbelt nervously again.

From her bag, she took out the icon and held it in both hands. Once, she'd have had rosary beads buried in the bottom of her bag. Her mother's old wooden ones, worn down from years of praying. Jessica no longer went to Mass on Sundays and holy-days, and she didn't use rosary beads. They were at home in her bedside drawer, discarded. What had God done for her exactly?

Susie held on to the arm-rests for the first swooping movement of the turbulence. It wasn't

63

too bad, she thought, as her stomach stopped rolling. She chanced a smile at Chloe.

'I'm glad we didn't go out last night,' Chloe said, trying to joke. 'We'd be in bits now –'

She didn't finish the sentence. The plane swooped again before jerking upwards with ferocity. Susie realised that if this was real turbulence, then she'd never experienced it before. This wasn't a mildly bumpy ride. This was like the biggest rollercoaster she'd ever been on. She held her breath, wishing it was all over. Pilots knew how to avoid turbulence these days, didn't they?

And then came another dive, worse than the previous one. The plane righted itself.

Nobody spoke. And then, a woman screamed. It was like a signal allowing everyone to yell. Loud sobs could be heard, all the small children on the flight seemed to start crying at the same time. And above it all, one woman's loud voice, like a mourner at a funeral.

'Help us! Help us!'

'This is some rollercoaster,' said Pat with bravado.

Claire was rigid with fear beside him. 'Shut up,' she wanted to say. 'This is terrifying, we're all going to die.' But she said nothing because her voice didn't work any more.

She had never known such fear. The plane

dived like a whale in the sea, and then jerked up again endlessly. Bits of luggage rolled up and down the aisles. Though she clung to Anthony's hand tightly, it wasn't enough. Even he couldn't save them.

She thought of recent plane crashes and an article she'd seen in the paper about thunderstorms, turbulence and crashes. She hadn't read the article, but it must have been a sad story. Papers didn't print good news. It was clear: they were going to die. All she could think of were her babies. The babies she dreamed about. At least they weren't with her now. It would be unbearable to have them sit with her on a crashing plane and not be able to save them.

Jessica didn't get to the airsickness bag in time. She threw up on to the seat beside her. She didn't care. Pure terror raced through her. The plane swooped and shuddered again. Every time it nosed up, it seemed to nose down again into a more frightening loop. Down, dragging her stomach with it, then up with horrifying speed.

The screaming was getting worse. It sounded like someone beside her was shrieking 'no'. And then Jessica realised it was her own voice. No, no, she didn't want to die.

\* \* \*

'Why aren't they telling us anything?' demanded Anthony hoarsely.

Despite her panic, Claire thought the flight crew were probably all just as terrified as the passengers. She could see the top of one of the stewardess' heads as she sat in her seat. She wished she could see the woman's face. *Was she scared? Was this normal?*

At that moment, something clicked over her head and the oxygen mask dangled in front of her eyes. All along the plane, terrified people reached for the hanging masks and put them on.

'The cabin hasn't lost pressure, you do not need your mask,' went an anxious announcement, but nobody listened.

This was it, everyone thought: we're going to crash.

And then the swooping stopped. The plane made a few mild judders and calmed. Claire sat as still as she could in her seat, afraid her movement might start the plane rocking again. But no.

The public address system pinged on.

'This is Captain Ryan speaking.' He sounded calm, as if nothing had happened.

'Sorry about that,' he said. 'We were warned of some turbulence, but we didn't expect it to be that bad. It was a bumpy ride. The cabin crew will shortly be moving among you, checking everyone's all right.'

'Typical,' said Pat. 'Make it all sound like a blip and none of us will sue.'

Claire shot him a look of dislike. 'We're all right,' she said. 'That's all that matters. How can you talk about suing anyone?'

'But look at what we went through,' said Pat. 'We need compensation for that.'

'Oh, shut up, Pat,' yelled Tricia. 'Claire's right, we're safe.'

Humbled, Pat began to mumble about how he was 'only saying . . .'

He reached down and hauled up his brandy bottles. Miraculously, neither of them was broken. 'I don't care if we're not supposed to drink our duty-free on the plane,' he said. 'I reckon after that ride, I need a snifter.'

Claire's pulse was still racing and yet when Pat unscrewed the bottle, her heart began to slow down. It was as if everything was in slow motion. She watched Pat take a huge gulp of the raw liquor, and then another. He wiped the top of the bottle with his hand and passed it across her to Anthony, man to man. She watched Anthony's hand grab the bottle and saw him raise it to his lips. His eyes were shut as he drank. But the change in him was like watching the sun go behind clouds. He drank great gulps, as if he was thirsty and it was water instead of brandy.

'Leave a drop for me,' said Pat in alarm. And then added, 'Ah, I suppose I have another bottle, after all.' He reached for the second bottle and started on that.

Claire clicked her seatbelt off and hauled herself out past Pat.

'The seatbelt sign is still on,' said a pale-faced stewardess when Claire reached the toilets.

'Sorry,' said Claire, 'I'm going to throw up.'

The light in the toilets was bright. Everything looked astonishingly real. Even the scent of chemical loo stuff was strangely wonderful. Life was still hers. Somehow, the plane hadn't plummeted to the ground.

Was this the born-again feeling people had after a near-death experience?

She felt so very alive. And sad at the same time.

She'd clung to Anthony's hand as the plane had swooped. She'd thought that being together was the only important thing at that moment. But for Anthony, the only important thing had been the brandy. He hadn't turned to her to kiss her when the plane stopped diving. He'd turned to Pat's bottle. He always would.

*   *   *

Jessica could smell the stench of her own vomit and yet she didn't care. Human beings threw up, the same way babies pooped in nappies. It was the way of the world. Life and death. Life was precious.

The woman behind her was still screaming. Jessica stood up, turned around and tried to comfort her.

'It's all right,' she said calmly.

Two teenage girls sat beside the woman, holding her hands tightly and looking shocked at their mother's behaviour.

'We're going to be fine now. The captain said so,' Jessica said calmly.

The woman still screamed.

'Slapping might help,' said one of the girls.

'Just a little slap,' Jessica agreed.

The slap startled the woman into silence.

'We're fine now,' Jessica said again.

The woman started to cry instead. 'That's better,' Jessica said to the girls. 'If you have something sweet to drink, like lemonade, that would be good for you all. Sugar helps.'

A Diet Coke was produced and they all had some.

'I've a Mars bar,' said the younger daughter.

She broke it into four bits. Jessica had never tasted anything so wonderful.

'When we land, I'm going to buy ten of these,' she said fervently.

'Me too,' said the younger girl. 'I was on a diet, but what's the point of being thin if you're dead, right?'

Finally, the woman seemed to come out of her trance. 'Thank you,' she mumbled to Jessica. She hugged her daughters. 'It was awful, I thought we were going to die.'

For some reason, Sarah's remark about how you never knew what was around the corner came into Jessica's mind. It had been a turbulent plane instead of a ten-ton truck. The effect had been the same: the plane journey had shaken something out of Jessica's mind for good.

She thought of getting home with her ten Mars bars and sitting down in her own living room. She imagined picking up her phone and calling her beloved sons to tell them about her plane journey. She had a lot to live for.

Chloe held her hand out and watched it vibrate.

'I can't stop shaking,' she said. 'I'm so thirsty, too. Do you think they'll come round with the drinks again?'

Tea, thought Susie. I want a nice cup of tea in my kitchen with Mum and Dad and Finn.

And a pizza takeaway, and maybe we could all watch a DVD afterwards, something soothing.

'I'd love a cup of tea,' she said.

Chloe looked up the aisle. The cabin crew were trying to calm people who were still upset. The air stank of vomit and spilled drinks. She didn't think the tea trolley would be top priority for a while.

'Should we get up and make tea ourselves?' she suggested. 'I've always wanted a go of the trolley.'

Susie looked at her and they both giggled. They weren't sure why, but suddenly they were laughing so much that Susie's stomach hurt.

'That's so funny,' shrieked Chloe.

'I know!' roared Susie.

'You know what? We're alive!!' Chloe yelled suddenly.

Behind them, someone clapped.

'We're alive!!' shouted someone else.

It was like a football chant running down the cabin. 'We're alive.'

'Do you know what I'm going to do when I land?' Susie said when she'd stopped laughing.

'Kiss the ground, the way the last Pope did?' Chloe asked. ''Cos that's what I'm going to do.'

Susie grinned. 'No, I'm going to tell Finn about Lucas.'

'You're kidding me, right?'

'I'm not kidding. I thought of it when we were going up and down, that I love Finn so much and I want him to know me, the good and the bad of me. And if he can't deal with that, then we shouldn't be together.'

'Did the turbulence wreck your brain?'

'Actually, it fixed it. We could have died, Chloe. Think about it. We only get one chance at life, so let's do it right.'

'What's that got to do with telling your fiancé you slept with another man?'

'I don't know why you never thought about a career in law,' Susie grumbled. 'I can see you doing the whole "case for the prosecution" thing.'

Chloe laughed.

'I'm going to be a stewardess, remember?' she said, and they both laughed again.

'Oh, go on, tell Finn the truth,' Chloe said. 'We nearly died, after all. If he can't forgive you now, there's no hope for you.'

Getting off the plane, Anthony held on to Pat's brandy bottle as if it were a lifebuoy.

'You're my mate, Pat,' he said, walking alongside his new best friend.

Claire had to help Tricia with the kids. Millie was now asleep in her mother's arms after her terrifying ordeal. Fiona was silent. She held Claire's hand and didn't utter a word. She was clearly traumatised.

'You can't blame them for having a drink,' Tricia said, trying to carry all the children's things along with her own carry-on case. Laden-down, the two women followed their swaying husbands.

Claire didn't answer that. She actually blamed herself for thinking Anthony could change. He might want to, but he wasn't strong enough. It was that simple.

Concerned airport staff greeted the passengers.

'You should talk to them,' Claire said to Tricia. 'Perhaps they have some advice on what to do about the children. That must have been so frightening for them.'

Tricia nodded and hugged Millie closer to her.

One group of people were boldly demanding 'What about compensation? Was the plane faulty? Was that why the oxygen masks came down?' As if compensation would help.

Claire avoided them. Incredibly, nobody was hurt and nobody had suffered a heart attack. She had no time for people who expected financial profit for every bit of misery. Life hurt. There was no compensation for that, right?

The terrifying flight would probably make the next day's papers. Some of the angry passengers were busily phoning newspapers, talking to reporters about what had happened.

Anthony and Pat were making drunken plans to meet up soon for a drink.

'We'll never forget each other after this,' Anthony said. He gave Pat a thump on the back.

'No, never,' Pat agreed.

Claire pulled Anthony and his bottle away from Pat.

'Let's go,' she said quietly, but with steel in her voice. She told the airport staff that she and her husband were fine, and they set off across the airport for the baggage reclaim area.

Jessica walked off the plane with her three new friends, the teenage girls and their mother.

'I'm glad Dad wasn't on the plane,' the younger girl explained. 'He had a heart attack last year and he might have had one on the plane, don't you think?'

'He might have,' Jessica said. 'But he wasn't on the plane. We were and we're safe. All's well that ends well. You'll have something interesting

74

to write in essays when you go back to school,' she added. 'Do you still do those "What I did on my summer holidays" essays?'

Both girls laughed.

'No,' said the older girl. 'We have to do boring ones about global warming, or "Is nuclear energy the future or the past?"'

Jessica grinned. 'They're both pretty awful,' she said. 'What you did on your summer holidays sounds much better.'

A member of the ground staff came up to them and spoke to Jessica.

'Madam, how are you?' She took Jessica's hands and led her to a chair as if she were an old lady.

'I'm fine,' said Jessica. 'Nothing wrong with me that a good cup of tea wouldn't cure. Or,' she smiled at the teenage girls, 'a Mars bar.'

'I think I've aged. Doesn't something scary make you age? Like making your hair turn white?' Chloe was in the ladies toilet peering at her face in the mirror. 'See, look.' She pointed at a minuscule wrinkle. 'That wasn't there yesterday.'

'Oh my God yes! You're deformed!' said Susie, leaning close.

'Cow,' said Chloe, pushing her away.

'Smoking and sunbathing make you age,' Susie

said, 'which is exactly what we've been doing for the past two weeks, so we've only ourselves to blame.'

'That only happens to old people,' Chloe said coolly. 'I'd love a cigarette now. Hurry up and let's get our bags. I want to have a fag outside.'

Anthony had filed the long-term car park number in the diary section of his mobile phone. But somewhere between getting off the plane and getting on to the bus to the car park at Dublin airport, he'd lost his phone.

He slowly searched his pockets again on the bus. 'Dunno,' he said and hiccupped. 'Dunno where it went.'

Claire didn't lose her temper with him. She knew she had to keep her anger inside. It was too huge to let out.

In the end, she asked the car park attendant which part of the car park had been open the day they'd left.

He consulted a colleague on the phone. 'Area K,' he said.

'K! That's it!' said Anthony happily. 'I knew I'd remember it if someone told me.'

He waited with the suitcases while Claire found the car and drove back to him.

'Sorry,' he said, suddenly gazing at her with his big sad eyes.

Claire didn't want to heal the pain inside them any more.

Sometimes when he drank, she tried to take the bottle away from him. Today, she let him finish the brandy as they drove across the city to Bray. Everything in the car reeked of alcohol. Claire couldn't wait to get home to shower and change. But not yet.

Anthony dozed and only woke up when Claire stopped the car.

'My mum's house!' he said, pleased.

He was so drunk, he'd be delighted if she'd brought him to a top-security prison, Claire decided.

Anthony's father, Larry, answered the door. He was surprised to see his son and daughter-in-law.

'The plane nearly crashed,' Anthony said merrily, throwing his arms round his father.

Larry's eyes met Claire's.

'It was a terrible flight,' Claire said. 'Anthony's been drinking.'

'Just a little bottle,' Anthony said, waving the big, empty brandy bottle. He lifted it to his lips but there was nothing left.

His mother, Reenie, came out of the kitchen

at that moment. She was wearing an apron and the smell of roast chicken followed her. Her face fell when she saw how drunk Anthony was.

Claire went back to the car and pulled out her husband's suitcase. His was always smaller than hers. She remembered the good-humoured joking when they were packing to go to Corfu. Her heart ached, but she couldn't go back now.

She'd seen what Tricia had settled for. Pat was opening a bottle when he should have been comforting his daughters after the turbulence. His first thought had been for himself. Perhaps he wasn't as much of a drinker as Anthony was, but he'd get there in the end. Claire could cope with that for herself, but not for her daughters or her sons. She wanted children. She wanted a husband.

'What are you doing?' asked Reenie when she saw Claire holding Anthony's suitcase.

'What do you think?' said Larry to his wife.

Reenie sat down on a chair and buried her face in her hands.

'I'm sorry, Reenie,' said Claire. 'I can't live like this any more. I don't want our marriage to come second to a bottle every time.'

'He could go to rehab,' Reenie said eagerly.

'That would be great,' Claire agreed.

'He won't do that,' Larry pointed out. 'I told

him we'd get the money together somehow, but he said he couldn't bear to go to one of those places. Then I told him about my old friend who went to Alcoholics Anonymous. He says he'd have gone back drinking if it wasn't for AA. But Anthony said he didn't like that idea either. Said he could do it himself. I don't think he's ready to stop.'

Claire nodded. She didn't think Anthony was ready to stop either.

As she drove away, she wondered why she didn't feel guilty about leaving Anthony. It was something to do with the plane journey, she realised. Until then, she'd felt responsible for her husband. It was her job to take care of him. To *fix* him. She had thought she could fix his alcoholism. But she couldn't.

People had so little power, she realised with stunning clarity. The plane had taught her that. Except for the pilot, nobody on the flight had any power over the turbulence. Even the pilot was helpless at first.

It was entirely out of their hands whether they lived or died.

She hadn't failed Anthony by walking away. She was merely accepting that she wasn't able to fix him. She could only fix herself.

She felt sorry about the lovely Athena Hotel.

It had been so beautiful, an oasis at the end of her marriage. She'd thought she and Anthony could go there again sometime, but now, she knew she would never go back. Never mind. Instead, she would go forward.

Jessica's hall was awash with junk mail when she pushed open the front door. So much for cancelling the post in case burglars knew she was away, she thought with a grin. Everything was exactly as she'd left it. Her few houseplants had all survived, thanks to being left in the bath with wet towels under them.

The back garden was suitably overgrown. Jessica didn't mind that either. She was in the mood for some vigorous weeding. In fact, she thought she might visit the garden centre the next day and buy a few plants. The lavender was very woody and could do with being replaced, and the flower beds needed a bit of colour in them. They were probably giving away bedding plants like petunias this late in the season.

She changed out of her stained travel clothes, showered and put on her pyjamas.

After she'd unpacked, she phoned Marty in Cork and told him about the awful flight.

'Mum, that sounds terrible. Are you really

okay?' he asked. 'Do you want me to come to Dublin to see you?'

'No,' she said, 'although I might come to visit you.'

She'd only been to see him once since Jack's death. On that visit, she'd kept crying as she thought how proud Marty's father would have been to see him doing so well.

'That would be brilliant,' said Marty happily.

Next, she texted Liam in Australia to tell him she was home. She signed it with kisses and a little yellow smiley face. She'd never done that before, but she wanted to show Liam how much better she was feeling.

Then she made herself a cup of tea and wandered round the house. The house wasn't different. Every bit of it still reminded her of Jack. But she was different. Stronger.

The plan she'd made before she went to Corfu wouldn't be necessary. Upstairs in her bathroom, she found the container of pills. There were ones left over from when Jack was dying: sleeping pills, anti-anxiety pills and very strong painkillers. Jessica had decided that if she took them all and washed them down with paracetamol, then she was sure to die. It had seemed like a good plan at the time. She wanted to escape the pain of living.

That was before Corfu and the flight home. She'd thought she wanted to die, but it turned out, she hadn't. When the plane had been diving in the sky, Jessica had realised she wanted to live. She simply hadn't known how to live without Jack. There was a difference.

She put the pills in a bag. She'd take them to the pharmacy tomorrow to let the chemist get rid of them. It might be dangerous to wash them down the loo.

Then she climbed into the double bed with her gardening magazines.

'I have great plans for the garden, Jack,' she said out loud. 'You're going to love looking down on it. What do you think about hydrangea bushes?'

Susie phoned Finn as soon as they were on the bus leaving the airport.

'You should have told me you'd landed,' Finn said. 'I wanted to come and pick you up.'

'Well, it was all a bit messy because there was a lot of turbulence on our flight and we were met by airport ground staff to make sure we were all right,' Susie said. She told him the whole story.

'We thought we were going to die,' yelled Chloe into the phone.

'I'll meet you at the bus stop beside the hotel,' Finn said grimly.

'Why did you say we thought we were going to die?' demanded Susie when she hung up.

'Because we did. Besides, it's better if Finn thinks you almost died,' Chloe said. 'Then he might not be so cross with you for going to bed with someone else.'

A woman on the bus turned to look at them and said, 'It sounds like the pair of you had one hell of a holiday.'

'Oh, we did,' said Chloe. 'It was wild.'

Finn was standing there, looking anxious, when they got off the bus.

As soon as Finn hugged her, Susie began to cry.

'It must have been terrible,' Finn said, clinging to her.

Susie cried more. She wasn't crying over the turbulence.

'Give me the car keys and tell me where you parked,' demanded Chloe.

'Why?' asked Finn.

'Just do it,' Susie added.

She took the two suitcases and hauled them over to the hotel car park where Finn's car was parked.

'What's going on?' Finn asked Susie when they were alone. He wasn't stupid.

'I slept with someone on holiday,' Susie said

straight out. Might as well get it over with. If he wanted to leave her, he would. She couldn't bear the waiting. 'I love you and it was a mistake, but I had to tell you.'

Finn's freckled face was heartbroken, but he wasn't sobbing. And he wasn't looking at her with disgust. Not yet.

'I thought girls kept things like that to themselves,' he said, and his voice was hard.

'I'm not "girls". I've never done anything like this before and it was a mistake,' Susie said. 'I'm telling you because I don't want secrets between us. When the plane was going through the turbulence, we did think we were going to die. The oxygen masks even fell down. Although the pilot said that was a mistake. I realised I didn't want to start married life by lying to you.'

There. She'd said it all.

'Why?' he asked.

It was the one question to which Susie had no answer. She still didn't know why she'd slept with Lucas.

'You know what, you and Chloe take the car. I'll get it later.' Finn's face was dark now.

'But . . .' began Susie.

'No,' he shouted. 'Take it. You can leave the keys in the office for me. Put them in an envelope. I don't want to see you.'

He turned away from her and walked off, head down.

Susie watched him go. There was nothing she could do or say to stop him.

She didn't even cry any more. She just felt numb.

'It didn't go so well, then?' said Chloe.

Susie slumped into the driver's seat of Finn's car. It was only a few years old, miles nicer and cleaner than her old banger. Finn kept it very tidy. She burst into tears again.

Chloe handed her a tissue.

A week went by and Susie's Greek tan began to fade. She lost weight too. She didn't feel hungry. Her work clothes began to feel loose.

'Could we write a book about "The Break-Up Diet"?' said Chloe, trying to make her laugh.

'No, we'd have to call it "The Stupid Cow Diet",' Susie said sadly.

That Friday, she left the office late. Everyone else had gone to Maguire's Pub for Friday-evening drinks. Susie had nothing to celebrate. Everyone knew that she and Finn had split up. At least he hadn't mentioned why. He was a gentleman, Chloe said.

'Any other guy would tell everyone,' she said.

'I know,' Susie agreed.

She walked through the car park to her car and suddenly Finn was standing in front of her. He looked thinner too. And pale.

'Hi,' he said.

'Hi,' she said nervously. 'How have you been?'

Finn took a step towards her. 'Miserable,' he said.

Susie felt warmth rise up inside her. 'Miserable without me?' she said hopefully.

He nodded. 'I don't want to know about it,' he said. 'Not now, not ever.'

'I'm so sorry,' she said, reaching out.

Finn opened his arms and Susie went into them. 'I love you,' she said. She buried her face in his jacket.

'I love you too.'

'Do you still want to get married?' she asked.

'Do you?' he asked.

She wasn't able to speak. Instead, her eyes brimming with tears, she nodded.

'OK,' Finn said. 'I should tell you that my mother has decided profiteroles are out and we should have mini cupcakes instead.'

Susie felt the tears fall down her cheeks. A month ago, she'd have groaned at the thought of his mother. Now, she didn't care. It was Finn she was marrying. His mother could have whatever she wanted. Susie had what she wanted.

Now that she'd nearly lost it, she understood how precious it was.

'Cupcakes sound fine to me,' she mumbled, holding him close.

# Quick Reads

## Books in the Quick Reads series

# Quick Reads

## Short, sharp shots of entertainment

As fast and furious as an action film. As thrilling as a theme park ride. Quick Reads are short sharp shots of entertainment – brilliantly written books by bestselling authors and celebrities. Whether you're an avid reader who wants a quick fix or haven't picked up a book since school, sit back, relax and let Quick Reads inspire you.

We would like to thank all our partners in the Quick Reads project for their help and support:

Arts Council England
The Department for Business, Innovation and Skills
NIACE
unionlearn
National Book Tokens
The Reading Agency
National Literacy Trust
Welsh Books Council
Basic Skills Cymru, Welsh Assembly Government
The Big Plus Scotland
DELNI
NALA

Quick Reads would also like to thank the Department for Business, Innovation and Skills; Arts Council England and World Book Day for their sponsorship and NIACE for their outreach work.

Quick Reads is a World Book Day initiative.
www.quickreads.org.uk                    www.worldbookday.com

# Other resources

Free courses are available for anyone who wants to develop their skills. You can attend the courses in your local area. If you'd like to find out more, phone 0800 66 0800.

A list of books for new readers can be found on www.firstchoicebooks.org.uk or at your local library.

Publishers Barrington Stoke (www.barringtonstoke.co.uk) and New Island (www.newisland.ie) also provide books for new readers.

The BBC runs an adult basic skills campaign. See www.bbc.co.uk/raw.

www.quickreads.org.uk          www.worldbookday.com

# What's next?

Tell us the name of an author you love

| Cathy Kelly | Go ▶ |

and we'll find your next great book.